*To all the children who
feel like they aren't enough ...*

*We are all missing something.
No one has everything.*

*Learning to cope with what you
are missing in life will make
you strong.*

*And then helping other people
will make you enough.*

Go for it.

Published in 2013 in Great Britain by
Barrington Stoke Ltd
18 Walker Street, Edinburgh, EH3 7LP

www.barringtonstoke.co.uk

This story was first published in a different form in
Wow! 366, Scholastic Children's Books, 2008

Text © 2008 Georgia Byng
Illustrations © Mike Phillips

Individual ISBN 978-1-78112-303-4
Pack ISBN 978-1-78112-308-9

Not available separately

Printed in China by Leo

www.barringtonstoke.co.uk

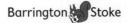

Pancake Face

Georgia Byng

Illustrated by Mike Phillips

Alice Peasbody lived in Victorian times.

Her nickname was 'Pancake Face'. She didn't have a nose.

It might have been all right to have no nose, but people did point, and snigger, and look at Alice with horror.

Alice began to wear a hood and keep away from people.

One day Alice asked the doctor for a
pretend nose.

The pretend nose was attached to a pair of glasses. The whole thing was very clever. The china nose rubbed on Alice's flat face, but when it was on, Alice felt more normal, and so she wore it.

When Alice was 16, she went to work in an office in the city. Life was better. No one knew that Alice had no nose. She chose a desk in a dark corner and kept herself to herself.

The office block had a roof garden where birds came to sing. Only the birds knew Alice's secret. When she was alone in the sun, she would take off her glasses. Of course, the nose came off too.

Five years passed.

One day a handsome man with a sunny nature came to work in the office. He was called Mr Coram and he made everyone laugh.

But Alice kept to the shadows, in case Mr Coram saw her pretend nose.

Alice grew very unhappy. Who would ever
love a Pancake Face?

The only times Alice was happy were when she was near Mr Coram, or when she was on the roof with the birds.

One warm summer evening, Alice was on the roof when Mr Coram surprised her.

Alice's glasses were on the bench!

As Mr Coram walked over, Alice reached
for her glasses. But she knocked them. Her
no-nose disguise clattered to the ground.

"It's lovely in the sun, isn't it?" Mr Coram said.

He sat on the bench across from Alice.

"Lovely," Alice said. "Atishoo!" She pretended to sneeze and held a hankie to her face.

Mr Coram rubbed his eye. Then Alice's mouth fell open. Mr Coram had pulled his eye out of the socket!

"People used to call me Cyclops," Mr Coram said. His one eye twinkled. "What did they call you, Alice?"

"They called me P-P-Pancake Face," Alice
said.

Alice and Mr Coram began a toy company a
year later.

They called it 'False Faces for Fun'.

And what about Alice and Mr Coram's own
false faces?

They never wore them again.

Are you NUTS about stories?

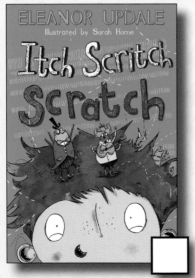

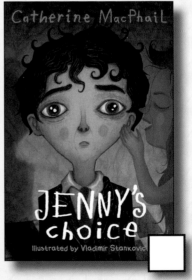

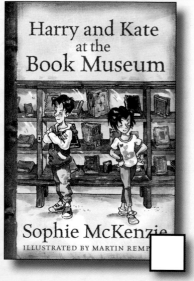

Read ALL the Acorns!